Park Stories: *Richmond Park*

Park Stories: The Running of the Deer
© Shena Mackay 2009

ISBN: 978-0-9558761-6-5

Series Editor: Rowan Routh

Published by The Royal Parks
www.royalparks.org.uk

Production by Strange Attractor Press
BM SAP, London, WC1N 3XX, UK
www.strangeattractor.co.uk

Cover design: Ali Hutchinson

Park Stories devised by Rowan Routh

Shena Mackay has asserted her moral right to be identified as the author of this work in accordance with the Copyright, Designs and Patents Act, 1988.

All rights reserved. No part of this publication may be reproduced in any form or by any means without the written permission of the publishers. A CIP catalogue record for this book is available from the British Library.

The Royal Parks gratefully acknowledges the financial support of Arts Council England.

Printed by Kennet Print, Devizes, UK on 100% post-consumer recycled Cyclus offset paper using vegetable-based inks.

The Running of the Deer

Shena Mackay

THE
ROYAL
PARKS

The Running of the Deer

As the pair of shire horses, harnessed together, dragged a tree trunk across the horizon, in the lull following the morning rush hour of commuter traffic, bicycles and school-run vehicles, Richmond Park settled back into its ancient aspect. Some of the oak trees, grown from medieval acorns, had been standing here long before the land was walled and made into a royal hunting park. The horses, silhouetted against a gauzy November sky which leached the colour from the trees and the birds and the airy globes of mistletoe in their branches, passed from sight and the landscape momentarily belonged to itself and its innumerable non-human population. That is, until the palest smudge of sun burned through the grey and, just as if a wet brush had touched the page of a child's magic painting book, faint tints appeared and deepened. At that moment, a lanky figure in a flapping black coat entered the park through the Richmond Gate and strode up Queens Road which stretched empty in front of him.

On either side of the road groups of fallow deer and red deer grazed in the bleached tussocks or lay in the bracken among fallen branches scattered like discarded antlers which, twisted, polished, bleached, decaying, provided homes and sustenance for their thousands of tiny residents. Ever alert, the deer raised their heads as the man passed but no sentinel gave the signal to run as he loped on, apparently not noticing them or the shrill squadron of ring-necked parakeets, flashing sudden vermilion and crimson and scarlet above his head, or the lumbering green kite which fell from the windless sky, almost garrotting him. He was grasping a heavy shopping bag, and from time to time he groaned aloud and swung the bag backwards, smiting himself across the shoulders. Either he was unaware of his bizarre behaviour, or he thought he was quite alone. But somebody was watching him, concealed in the wooded slope on his right-hand side.

There goes The Poet, she thought, flagellating himself like some medieval penitent. With a supermarket carrier bag. What could the poet have done, she wondered, to deserve such self-punishment? Had he committed a horrible crime, leaving behind the body of some poor woman, was he just atoning for a night of dissipation, or was his anguish simply the outward expression of an internal artistic turmoil? Clare Carnevale, who was a freelance photographer working on a project of her own in the park – a pictorial diary of a year in its life – had observed this man several times and, struck by his dark and somewhat haggard looks, had decided that he must be a poet. Despite her practical appearance, professional waistcoat bristling with pockets, binoculars and cameras, Clare was of a romantic and archaic turn of mind, and now she pictured the poet fleeing from a tableau which might have come from a Victorian painting, wherein an abandoned wife, or mistress, stood distraught in a tumbledown cottage, with wide-eyed hungry children clinging to her skirts.

Clare, a small, brown woman in her late thirties, lived alone by choice in a bijou residence near the river. The cottage had come down through the family from her great-grandmother, a doughty widow with seventeen children, who earned her living as a rat-catcher. It was damp and cluttered with her photographic paraphernalia and books, the walls a jumble of sepia family portraits and her own work. She was happy there, occasionally entertaining family and friends, turning a blind eye, out of ancestral guilt, to any rodents she came across indoors or in her little garden. The things which gave her most pleasure in life were all visual; she loved the dappled coats of the deer and the way they fold and unfold their legs, the parakeets, and tiny brown birds with dabs of red lacquer and slicks of yellow paint on crests and wings, and the staccato gait of crows; she loved convoluted and tortuous roots and branches which swept down to the ground in sheltering needle-strewn caves, tree stumps vivid with emerald green starry moss, russet and tawny colours, and her heart beat faster at the sight of scarlet berries, flaming leaves reflected in the dark brimming water of the ponds, fly agarics, and the little jellified toadstools like sea-anemones which she had found this morning – and cherry blossom and cold spring flowers such as primroses, wood anemones, violets and sheets of bluebells, and cow parsley – each season took her by surprise yearly, as forgotten plants emerged again – and sometimes it was all too much and she felt as if her heart would burst.

As she went about her business, though, she 'collected' interesting-looking strangers, in the street and the supermarket and the park, unknown to themselves, and gave them names, and so she peopled her life with acquaintances, such as Mr Bojangles the busker, the Mouse and his Child, a sad-faced father and his little boy, Blanche Dubois, Reynard the fox, Woody Woodpecker, Whitey the albino blackbird, the Monarch of the Glen, a particularly magnificent stag with a chandelier of antlers – and more. Clare loved them all at a distance and was always secretly cheered by seeing them, but today, watching The Poet, she felt uneasy. What was in that heavy shopping bag he was hitting himself with? Maybe he had weighted it, and filled his pockets, with stones and was making his way to one of the ponds in the Isabella Plantation to end it all. Perhaps he was heading, appropriately, for Gallows Pond.

Clare followed him at a distance, unsure of what she would do if he were to wade into the pond. Was it deep enough to drown a man? She imagined his heavy black coat absorbing the water and pulling him under, coots, moorhens, ducks and geese shrieking as she plunged in, mud gripping her legs and sucking her down, slimy roots lassoing her feet, the two of them splashing and wrestling in a desperate, ungainly, doomed struggle. If he *had* done some dark deed, might it not be kinder to let him make an end of it, or would that be robbing his victim and family of justice?

She was distracted from these thoughts by a creature, seemingly half-tree, half man, who emerged from a thicket, his bulky dun-coloured clothes and hair and beard matted with burrs and curly fronds and twigs. This person was one of Clare's collection and she longed to photograph him, thinking that perhaps he was some elemental spirit or even the *genius loci* of the park, but she was daunted by his baleful glare. She called him Tammylan, after a character in the Enid Blyton books *The Children of Cherry Tree Farm* and *Willow Farm*. Not meeting his eyes, she hurried on, following The Poet's rakish progress. It occurred to her that Enid Blyton was perhaps more scholarly than she was given credit for, and had based Tammylan's name on that of the legendary Tam Lin who was captured by the Queen of Elfland. Tammylan was a wild man of the woods, who befriended four London children who had come to live on a farm. He was good and kindly, nut-brown and blue-eyed, a woodcarver and naturalist who knew all there was to know about the birds and animals who loved and trusted him. How many parents nowadays, though, would be happy to let their children roam the countryside with a man who lived in a cave with a curtain of bracken and heather across its entrance?

Clare had seen her Tammylan talking to the shire horses over the fence of their pasture, reaching up to offer first one of them and then the other something from one of the many bags which hung about him. The horses bowed their great heads over the fence and graciously accepted his gift. Clare, who had been told this fact by the Park Manager whom she had met when she was photographing some of the children's activities at the Holly Lodge Centre, knew that the horses were called Jed and Forté. Formerly dray horses, they had been retired from their work at the Bass and Burton's and Young's Breweries and had exchanged the traffic of the streets for the park, where they were now employed on forestry work. Clare loved Jed and Forté more than almost anybody here, or anywhere else. It was not just their size which made them seem noble; anachronistic in both equine and human terms, powerless over their own lives and yet symbolic of the dignity of labour down the ages, Jed and Forté stood foursquare and totemic on their great hooves, stirring an inexplicable sense of loss in those who saw them.

More people were about now, joggers, the confederacy of dog-walkers who met up every day, in their striped hats and scarves, as disparate in breed as their pets; a mother with a buggy, talking on her mobile while ambling in the wake of a toddler who was crouched down examining something he, or she – the child was so muffled up it was impossible to tell – had found on the path. Such a pity, Clare thought, that we have to lose that ability to live in each moment, our infant curiosity and wonder at the world; as a photographer, she had retained it to some extent, after all, her *raison d'etre* was to capture and fix a unique minute, but she was always conscious of the passing of time.

Never more so than now, as she almost lost her target, who had struck out across the rusty bracken. Avoiding ant hills and a group of deer startled by a lone dog, she passed a pair of youngsters, heads linked by earpieces, whose school uniforms betrayed their truancy. Clare was of course, on account of her age, invisible to them and they almost bumped into her. One of the dog-walkers – she recognized his red woolly hat – had left his dog with the group and was hurrying towards the dog-free zone. She realized that The Poet, too, was making for Pembroke Lodge, the magnificent Georgian mansion overlooking the Thames. Clare slackened her pace, feeling slightly foolish and also a little disappointed that there was to be no watery drama after all.

She could have a cup of coffee at the cafeteria and then head for home. Or she might wander on up to Poet's Corner, in the hope of seeing again a flock of waxwings marauding the beautiful spindle tree growing beside the Rustic Panel commemorating the C18 poet James Thomson, who was known as 'the poet of *The Seasons*'. Most of his work was forgotten now, except for *Rule Britannia*, whose words he was assumed to have written. Thomson was born in Scotland but came to live in Richmond, and was buried in the churchyard nearby.

Clare decided to climb King Henry's Mound, the highest point in the park, from where, on a clearer day than this, you could look across London to St. Paul's Cathedral, and westwards to Windsor Castle. There was still a chance that she might encounter The Poet, although it seemed rather pointless now. He probably wasn't a poet at all, but the sort of person who looked at the deer and thought, 'Yum yum, venison!'

The sun had withdrawn, defeated, Clare was cold and her mood had soured.

How she hated Henry VIII, and how typical of him to have a mound on top of a prehistoric burial ground. It had been said that he stood there to see a rocket fired from the Tower of London, to signify the execution of Anne Boleyn, but it was also claimed that he had been in Wiltshire at the time. A feeble alibi, if ever there was one. Clare walked round the perimeter of Pembroke Lodge behind a mother and daughter, arm-in-arm, who were casing the joint, picking their way over faded confetti mixed with leafy detritus, discussing whether it would be the right venue for a wedding reception two years hence.

'You have to picture it in summer', said the mother, consulting a booklet, 'the laburnum walk and all the lovely irises – you could have your napkins themed to fit in with the flowers. Champagne on the terrace with superb views over Kingston and Ham!'

'A view of ham?' said the daughter, dully.

'Oh, how fascinating', her mother went on, 'apparently the lodge used to be an old molecatcher's cottage in the olden days, before it had a make-over. And Bertrand Russell lived here as an orphan.'

'Who?' said the daughter. 'I thought it was supposed to be the Countess of Pembroke? And what do you mean, "mole *catcher*?" Don't you have to have them removed?'

'And turkeys nested in these very trees!' offered the mother, as if she were playing her trump card.

'Well, *that's* not very appropriate for a summer wedding, turkeys, is it?'

The mother sighed heavily, and they moved out of earshot.

Clare walked towards the Ian Dury Bench, placed there in memory of the musician, who had loved the park. She thought she would sit for a moment, despite the cold. This interactive bench was solar-powered and you could plug in your own headphones and listen to some of Ian Dury's songs and his appearance on *Desert Island Discs*. But as Clare approached, she saw that it was occupied by a woman sobbing under the plaque which read 'Reasons To Be Cheerful'. She hovered awkwardly, but before she could speak, the dog-walker brushed past her and sat down. Clare, unnoticed, stepped aside.

She learned, through the broken words and hum of condolences, that the woman had been bereaved recently.

The Running of the Deer

That her dog Dylan had died, that she had made the decision to end his life, and that she could not be consoled.

'Jenny', said the man, putting his arm round the weeping woman, 'You mustn't grieve so. Dylan will be waiting for you at Rainbow Bridge.'

'Rainbow Bridge?' said Jenny, lifting a face all swollen and smeared with anguish.

'What do you mean?'

Clare listened as he described gently the iridescent bridge twixt earth and the animal heaven where our departed pets live in happiness and harmony. 'There is just one thing missing, though, from their blissful afterlife – us!! But when we cross over Rainbow Bridge, up go the ears, the tails wag nineteen to the dozen, our beloveds leap into our arms, and we are reunited once more.'

Clare dissolved in tears. Why had nobody ever told her about Rainbow Bridge? There were pets who had been waiting decades for her to arrive. Would they all come running to greet her? What about the goldfish? And Great Grandmother Carnevale? Would she have been transmogrified into a pied piper in a bombazine dress, leading a troupe of smiling rats in haloes?

There were no waxwings in the spindle tree but its fruits trembled on their delicate stems in the wind which had sprung up, displaying their orange seeds in lobes of glowing pinkish red and lifted her spirits. She was standing by the Rustic Panel, which was shaped rather like a church lychgate, reading the verse by John Heneage Jesse:

> *Ye who from London's smoke and turmoil fly,*
> *To seek a purer air and brighter sky,*
> *Think of the Bard who dwelt in yonder dell*
> *Who sang so sweetly what he loved so well...*

'Yes, but the poor old bard only lived to forty-eight!' said a voice behind her. 'Caught a fatal chill on a boating expedition.'

Clare turned. Standing there was The Poet – and Tammylan – both holding take-away cups of coffee.

'I think you know us both by sight', the Poet said, holding out his hand. 'James Thomson, by coincidence. Fellow Scot and poet, by coincidence too. But no relation. And this is – oh well...'

Tammylan was shuffling away.

The black coat was cashmere, she saw, and didn't, as she'd imagined, smell of mould. Nor was there a taint of stale wine on his breath. He was smiling. She was aware that her own face was pinched and puckered by the cold.

'Clare Carnevale'.

'I know – I've seen you. And your work. There's something I've been wanting to ask you...'

'And I you! If you don't mind... why were you groaning and beating yourself with your shopping bag this morning? Have you – I mean, is something terribly wrong?'

'Was I?' He sounded surprised, glancing down at his bag. 'No idea – just the usual morning failure and remorse, I suppose. Or worrying about school fees – I've got a boy at White Lodge, the Royal Ballet school.'

'Oh.'

'Maybe I was thinking about work – that's what I want to talk to you about. You see, I've got this idea, to do a kind of *Seasons*, like my namesake – though I suppose his *Castle of Indolence* is more appropriate in my case – sort of documenting a year in the park, the management, the flora and fauna, symbiosis, all that stuff – and I thought some illustrations might help. I wondered if you'd be interested in collaborating. Me doing the words, you the pictures...'
'Me doing the pictures, you the words', she almost-echoed him. 'I –'

She broke off as a frantic yelping, coming their

way, made them both whirl round.

A small white dog, all tangled up in a green box kite which dragged behind it, was lolloping along on three legs, now running in circles, biting at the ever-tightening string which tied its fourth leg, now trying to escape from the bouncing kite. A sudden gust of wind filled the kite, lifting it and the dog from the ground. Clare screamed, breaking into a run. But James Thomson was there first, and stretching out a long black arm, hooked the dog from the air. He set it down at her feet. Clare looked at him.

'OK', she said. 'I'll do it.'